HILAIRE BELLOC
CAUTIONARY VERSES

HILAIRE BELLOC
CAUTIONARY VERSES

Original illustrations *by* B.T.B.
Introduction and new
illustrations *by* Quentin Blake

JONATHAN CAPE
LONDON

CAUTIONARY VERSES
A JONATHAN CAPE BOOK 0224 03073 6

Published in Great Britain by Jonathan Cape,
an imprint of Random House Children's Books

This edition published 2004

1 3 5 7 9 10 8 6 4 2

RANDOM HOUSE CHILDREN'S BOOKS
61-63 Uxbridge Road, London W5 5SA
A division of the Random House Group Ltd

RANDOM HOUSE AUSTRALIA (PTY) LTD
20 Alfred Street, Milsons Point, Sydney,
New South Wales 2061, Australia

RANDOM HOUSE NEW ZEALAND LTD
18 Poland Road, Glenfield, Auckland 10, New Zealand

RANDOM HOUSE (PTY) LTD
Endulini, 5A Jubilee Road, Parktown 2193, South Africa

THE RANDOM HOUSE GROUP Limited Reg No. 954009
www.**kids**at**randomhouse**.co.uk

A CIP catalogue record for this book is available from the British Library

Printed and bound by Mackays of Chatham plc, Chatham, Kent

PUBLISHER'S NOTE

Although this book was first published in 1939, many of the poems and illustration
were written and drawn during the Victorian era and reflect some of the attitudes and
events of that period. After considerable discussion we have decided to preserve the
original text and B.T.B illustrations. An edition containing the pictures by
Nicolas Bentley is available from Everyman

CONTENTS

INTRODUCTION

by Quentin Blake

CAUTIONARY TALES FOR CHILDREN

Illustrated by B.T.B.

NEW CAUTIONARY TALES
Illustrated by Quentin Blake

THE BAD CHILD'S BOOK OF BEASTS
Illustrated by B.T.B.

MORE BEASTS FOR WORSE CHILDREN
Illustrated by B.T.B.

MORE PEERS
Illustrated by B.T.B.

A MORAL ALPHABET
Illustrated by B.T.B.

INTRODUCTION

Somehow or other, as a schoolboy in the suburbs of London during the War, I failed to encounter the writings of Hilaire Belloc. I think I missed several other children's classics too, until I was a teenager or even a young adult. Fortunately, with really good books it doesn't matter what age you are; and for me it didn't matter with Belloc. Take Jim, for instance:

> *Now just imagine how it feels*
> *When first your toes and then your heels,*
> *And then by gradual degrees,*
> *Your shins and ankles, calves and knees,*
> *Are slowly eaten, bit by bit.*
> *No wonder Jim detested it!*

It is, like so much of Belloc, immediately memorable; it's almost difficult *not* to learn it by heart. The verse is fluent, controlled; if it is doggerel it is a very subtle form of doggerel. And the relish in, 'No wonder Jim *detested* it!' Belloc obviously enjoys the sound of it, and springs a neat little surprise in using a word which is so positive and yet so beautifully understates the situation.

It's not surprising that these poems were so popular – popular ever since they were first published nearly a hundred years ago. But I can't help thinking that Belloc might have rather mixed feelings if he were able to come back and see to what a large extent his fame depends on them. After all, he earned his living by writing (and by talking) and he wrote an enormous amount – speeches, novels, history, biography;

books about religion and politics, France and Italy; even about sailing; but it is by these nonsensical books of verse that most of us know him.

I don't think it is altogether an accident. If you read some of Belloc's serious poetry for adults it helps to underline the reason. There are melancholy poems about his feelings for rural Sussex and boisterous ones about the pleasures of drink and drinking, but nowadays I think they seem rather half-hearted, perhaps trying too hard to look like poetry. By contrast the verses collected in this book are accurate and alert; like a voice speaking to you. They're not only easy to memorize; they also make you want to recite them.

When Lewis Carroll and Edward Lear were writing it was at the height of the Victorian era. Because they were writing for children – writing 'nonsense' – they could discreetly make fun of the manners and formalities of the time. By the time that Belloc came to write, the century was almost over; it could openly be made fun of. The note is struck by the title of Belloc's first book for children; one at which the Victorians would surely have looked askance: *The Bad Child's Book of Beasts* (1896).

The pretexts for the *Cautionary Tales* (1907) existed in those books that the Victorians seemed to specialize in; the ones in which children who disregard the admonitions of their parents are trampled to death by horses, drowned in torrents, and meet other similar unfortunate ends. It was in setting out to make fun of all this that Belloc came across something unusual; the humour of the *ruthless*.

> *For every time she shouted 'Fire!'*
> *They only answered 'Little Liar!'*
> *And therefore when her Aunt returned,*
> *Matilda, and the House, were Burned.*

It was not an entirely new discovery, and other people have tried their hand at it, before and since. But Belloc understood best how to do it, and made it delectable. The reason for this, I think, is that not only did Belloc have a wonderful facility of language, but also the ability within him to be both the heavy parent *and* the misbehaving child; both Franklin Hyde's belligerent uncle and the boy himself *carousing in the dirt.*

Something like the same abilities aided Belloc in another speciality; one that appeared in the very first of his books – the level-voiced assertion of facts that we all know are untrue. He tells us, for instance, that the bison's hair is sewn on with needle and thread, and that the tiger (like the yak) is just the thing as a companion for children. It's almost like a game, and it was in fact very much as a game that *The Bad Child's Book of Beasts* was begun: a collaboration for their own amusement while on holiday in Scandinavia, between the young Belloc and his friend Lord Basil Blackwood. When it appeared as a book, it was under the initials H.B. and B.T.B. Later on, with the publication of *Cautionary Tales*, Belloc emerged as H. Belloc, clearly the author; though B.T.B. never abandoned the semi-anonymity of his initials. Perhaps he felt that was more suitable to an aristocrat with a pen in hand.

I am always very interested in the way drawings go with words – both the way that the characters of the artist and the author relate to each other and the way that illustrations alter or illuminate a text. Thousands of people, ever since the *Cautionary Verses* were published, have grown up with the original B.T.B. drawings, and think of him as the ideal collaborator for Belloc. Author and artist obviously shared the same sense of humour – a sense of humour with an element of lunacy about it more common nowadays than it can have been then.

I think we have to admit that Belloc was more skilled at writing verse than B.T.B. was at drawing; but B.T.B.'s drawings have just the right sort of feel to them. It's noticeable if you look at *Punch* of that time that the drawings, though they are meant to be funny, are pretty straightforward, with lots of cross–hatching to make it clear that they have been drawn properly. B.T.B.'s drawings don't look at all like that.

I think I know where B.T.B.'s way of drawing found its origin. Not long ago, I bought several books of the drawings of the nineteenth–century French illustrator Caran d'Ache. He was a master of telling a humorous story in pictures, a truly visual art almost unknown in England at the time; and he drew with a confident economy of line that I think I can see Basil Blackwood admired. His drawings were able to suggest just the right atmosphere of farce – wildly eccentric people taking themselves very seriously – which B.T.B. needed for Belloc's verses.

There is one book of Belloc verses which is included in this volume for which Blackwood did not supply illustrations. This is *New Cautionary Tales*, originally published in 1930. It was while I was writing this introduction, and after I had written those words above about B.T.B., that the publisher asked me if I would do drawings for that other book. Well, there is perhaps something a bit daunting as well as delightful about being asked to lend one's own assistance to a star turn of a century ago; but I too like Caran d'Ache and story-telling pictures, and I like the way B.T.B. runs his pictures through the text, and the sense of lunacy in it all, and so I hope that what I've done will be enjoyable and worthy of the occasion.

But, of course, the real team here is H.B. and B.T.B. The haranguing tone of Belloc's words with the impromptu quality of Blackwood's drawings – their very idiosyncrasy – leave me with a sense of the books as of some odd, lively, but not quite explicable encounter. It may be that the contents of this collection – a sense of the ridiculous preserved with all its original flavour – are as much humorous books for adults as they are for children.

Fortunately we don't have to decide. If we want to we can simply follow the Reviewer whom Belloc put into his Moral Alphabet (1899):

> . . . *'No person' (says he)*
> *'Will be really content without purchasing three,*
> *'While a Parent will send for a dozen of more,*
> *'And strew them about on the Nursery Floor.'*

Whatever his feelings about the disproportionate contribution of these works to his immortality, I am sure that Belloc would be disappointed at anything less.

QUENTIN BLAKE

April 1993

CAUTIONARY TALES
FOR CHILDREN

Illustrated by B.T.B

INTRODUCTION

Upon being asked by a Reader whether the verses contained in this book were true.

And is it True? It is not True.
And if it were it wouldn't do,
For people such as me and you
Who pretty nearly all day long
Are doing something rather wrong.
Because if things were really so,
You would have perished long ago,
And I would not have lived to write
The noble lines that meet your sight,
Nor B. T. B. survived to draw
The nicest things you ever saw.

H. B.

Jim,

Who ran away from his Nurse, and was eaten by a Lion.

There was a Boy whose name was Jim;
His Friends were very good to him.
They gave him Tea, and Cakes, and Jam,
And slices of delicious Ham,
And Chocolate with pink inside,
And little Tricycles to ride,

And read him stories through and through,
And even took him to the Zoo –
But there it was the dreadful Fate
Befell him, which I now relate.

You know – at least you *ought* to know,
For I have often told you so –
That Children never are allowed
To leave their Nurses in a Crowd;

Now this was Jim's especial Foible,
He ran away when he was able,
And on this inauspicious day
He slipped his hand and ran away!
He hadn't gone a yard when –

Bang!

With open Jaws, a Lion sprang,
And hungrily began to eat
The Boy: beginning at his feet.

Now just imagine how it feels
When first your toes and then your heels,
And then by gradual degrees,
Your shins and ankles, calves and knees,
Are slowly eaten, bit by bit.

No wonder Jim detested it!
No wonder that he shouted "Hi!"
The Honest Keeper heard his cry,
Though very fat

he almost ran
To help the little gentleman.
"Ponto!" he ordered as he came
(For Ponto was the Lion's name),

"Ponto!" he cried, with angry Frown.
"Let go, Sir! Down, Sir! Put it down!"

The Lion made a sudden Stop,
He let the Dainty Morsel drop,
And slunk reluctant to his Cage,
Snarling with Disappointed Rage
But when he bent him over Jim,
The Honest Keeper's Eyes were dim.

The Lion having reached his Head,
The miserable Boy was dead!

When Nurse informed his Parents, they
Were more Concerned than I can say: –
His Mother, as She dried her eyes,
Said, "Well – it gives me no surprise,
He would not do as he was told!"
His Father, who was self-controlled,
Bade all the children round attend

To James' miserable end,
And always keep a-hold of Nurse
For fear of finding something worse.

Henry King,

Who chewed bits of String, and was early cut off in Dreadful Agonies.

The Chief Defect of Henry King
Was chewing little bits of String.

At last he swallowed some which tied
Itself in ugly Knots inside.

Physicians of the Utmost Fame
Were called at once; but when they came
They answered,

as they took their Fees,
"There is no Cure for this Disease.
Henry will very soon be dead."
His parents stood about his Bed
Lamenting his Untimely Death,
When Henry, with his Latest Breath,
Cried –

"Oh, my Friends, be warned by me,

That Breakfast, Dinner, Lunch and Tea
Are all the Human Frame requires . . ."
With that the Wretched Child expires.

Matilda,

Who told Lies, and was Burned to Death.

Matilda told such Dreadful Lies,
It made one Gasp and Stretch one's Eyes;

Her Aunt, who, from her Earliest Youth,
Had kept a Strict Regard for Truth,

Attempted to Believe Matilda:
The effort very nearly killed her,
And would have done so, had not She
Discovered this Infirmity.
For once, towards the Close of Day,
Matilda, growing tired of play,

And finding she was left alone,
Went tiptoe

              to the Telephone
And summoned the Immediate Aid
Of London's Noble Fire-Brigade.
Within an hour the Gallant Band
Were pouring in on every hand,
From Putney, Hackney Downs and Bow,
With Courage high and Hearts a-glow
They galloped, roaring through the Town,

"Matilda's House is Burning Down!"
Inspired by British Cheers and Loud
Proceeding from the Frenzied Crowd,
They ran their ladders through a score
Of windows on the Ball Room Floor;
And took Peculiar Pains to Souse
The Pictures up and down the House,

Until Matilda's Aunt succeeded
In showing them they were not needed
And even then she had to pay
To get the Men to go away!

It happened that a few Weeks later
Her Aunt was off to the Theatre
To see that Interesting Play
The Second Mrs. Tanqueray.

She had refused to take her Niece
To hear this Entertaining Piece:
A Deprivation Just and Wise
To Punish her for Telling Lies.
That Night a Fire *did* break out –

You should have heard Matilda Shout!
You should have heard her Scream and Bawl,
And throw the window up and call
To People passing in the Street –
(The rapidly increasing Heat
Encouraging her to obtain
Their confidence) – but all in vain!
For every time She shouted "Fire!"
They only answered "Little Liar!"

And therefore when her Aunt returned,
Matilda, and the House, were Burned.

Franklin Hyde,

Who caroused in the Dirt and was corrected by His Uncle.

His Uncle came on Franklin Hyde
Carousing in the Dirt.

He Shook him hard from Side to Side
And Hit him till it Hurt,

Exclaiming, with a Final Thud,
"Take that! Abandoned Boy!

For Playing with Disgusting Mud
As though it were a Toy!"

MORAL

From Franklin Hyde's adventure, learn
To pass your Leisure Time
In Cleanly Merriment, and turn
From Mud and Ooze and Slime
And every form of Nastiness –
But, on the other Hand,
Children in ordinary Dress
May always play with Sand.

Godolphin Horne,

Who was cursed with the Sin of Pride, and Became a Boot-Black.

Godolphin Horne was Nobly Born;
He held the Human Race in Scorn,
And lived with all his Sisters where
His father lived, in Berkeley Square.

And oh! the Lad was Deathly Proud!
He never shook your Hand or Bowed,
But merely smirked and nodded thus:

How perfectly ridiculous!
Alas! That such Affected Tricks
Should flourish in a Child of Six!
(For such was Young Godolphin's age).

Just then, the Court required a Page,
Whereat the Lord High Chamberlain

(The Kindest and the Best of Men),

He went good-naturedly and took
A Perfectly Enormous Book
Called *People Qualified to Be*
Attendant on His Majesty,
And murmured, as he scanned the list
(To see that no one should be missed),

"There's William
Coutts has got
the Flue,

And Billy Higgs would never do,

And Guy de Vere is far too
young,

And . . . wasn't D'Alton's Father hung?
And as for Alexander Byng! – . . .
I think I know the kind of thing,
A Churchman, cleanly, nobly born,
Come let us say Godolphin Horne?"

But hardly had he said a word
When Murmurs of Dissent were heard.
The King of Iceland's Eldest Son
Said, "Thank you! I am taking none!"
The Aged Duchess of Athlone
Remarked, in her sub-acid tone,
"I doubt if He is what we need!"
With which the Bishops all agreed;
And even Lady Mary Flood
(*So* Kind, and oh! so *really* good)
Said, "No! He wouldn't do at all,
He'd make us feel a lot too small."
The Chamberlain said,

                    ". . . Well, well, well!
No doubt you're right . . . One cannot tell!"

He took his Gold and Diamond Pen
And Scratched Godolphin out again.

So now Godolphin is the Boy
Who blacks the Boots at the Savoy.

Algernon,

Who played with a Loaded Gun, and, on missing his

Sister was reprimanded by his Father.

Young Algernon, the Doctor's Son,
Was playing with a Loaded Gun.

He pointed it towards his sister

Aimed very carefully,
but

Missed her!

His Father, who was
standing near

The Loud Explosion chanced to Hear,

And reprimanded Algernon
For playing with a Loaded Gun.

Hildebrand,

Who was frightened by a Passing Motor, and was brought to Reason.

"Oh, Murder! What was that, Papa!"

"My child, It was a Motor-Car,
A Most Ingenious Toy!

Designed to Captivate and Charm
Much rather than to rouse Alarm
In any English Boy.

"What would your Great Grandfather who
Was Aide-de-Camp to General Brue,

And lost a leg at Waterloo,

And

Quatre-Bras and

Ligny too!

44

And died at Trafalgar! –

What would he have remarked to hear
His Young Descendant shriek with fear,
Because he happened to be near
A Harmless Motor-Car!
But do not fret about it! Come!

We'll off to Town

And purchase some!"

Lord Lundy,

Who was too Freely Moved to Tears, and thereby ruined his Political Career.

Lord Lundy from his earliest years
Was far too freely moved to Tears.
For instance if his Mother said,
"Lundy! It's time to go to Bed!"
He bellowed like a Little Turk.

Or if his father Lord Dunquerque

Said "Hi!" in a Commanding Tone,
"Hi, Lundy! Leave the Cat alone!"
Lord Lundy, letting go its tail,
Would raise so terrible a wail

As moved

    His

        Grandpapa

            the

            Duke

To utter the severe rebuke:
"When I, Sir! was a little Boy,
An Animal was not a Toy!"

His father's Elder Sister, who
Was married to a Parvenoo,

Confided to Her Husband, "Drat!
The Miserable, Peevish Brat!
Why don't they drown the Little Beast?"
Suggestions which, to say the least,
Are not what we expect to hear
From Daughters of an English Peer.
His grandmamma, His Mother's Mother,

Who had some dignity or other,
The Garter, or no matter what,
I can't remember all the Lot!
Said "Oh! that I were Brisk and Spry
To give him that for which to cry!"
(An empty wish, alas! for she

Was Blind and nearly ninety-three).

The Dear old Butler

thought – but there!
I really neither know nor care
For what the Dear Old Butler thought!
In my opinion, Butlers ought
To know their place, and not to play
The Old Retainer night and day

I'm getting tired and so are you,
Let's cut the Poem into two!

*　　*　　*

Lord Lundy

(SECOND CANTO)

It happened to Lord Lundy then,
As happens to so many men:
Towards the age of twenty-six,
They shoved him into politics;
In which profession he commanded
The income that his rank demanded
In turn as Secretary for
India, the Colonies, and War.
But very soon his friends began
To doubt if he were quite the man:
Thus, if a member rose to say
(As members do from day to day),

"Arising out of that reply . . . !"

Lord Lundy would begin to cry.
A Hint at harmless little jobs
Would shake him with convulsive sobs.

While as for Revelations, these
Would simply bring him to his knees,
And leave him whimpering like a child.
It drove his Colleagues raving wild!
They let him sink from Post to Post,
From fifteen hundred at the most
To eight, and barely six – and then
To be Curator of Big Ben! . . .
And finally there came a Threat
To oust him from the Cabinet!

The Duke – his aged grand-sire – bore
The shame till he could bear no more.
He rallied his declining powers,
Summoned the youth to Brackley Towers,
And bitterly addressed him thus –
"Sir! you have disappointed us!
We had intended you to be
The next Prime Minister but three:
The stocks were sold; the Press was squared:
The Middle Class was quite prepared.

But as it is! . . . My language fails!

Go out and govern New South Wales!"

* * *

The Aged Patriot groaned and died:

And gracious! how Lord Lundy cried!

Rebecca,

Who slammed Doors for Fun and Perished Miserably.

A Trick that everyone abhors
In Little Girls is slamming Doors.
A

Wealthy Banker's

Little Daughter

Who lived in Palace Green, Bayswater
(By name Rebecca Offendort),
Was given to this Furious Sport.

She would deliberately go

And Slam the door like
Billy-Ho!

To make her

Uncle Jacob start.

She was not really bad at heart,
But only rather rude and wild:
She was an aggravating child . . .

It happened that a Marble Bust
Of Abraham was standing just
Above the Door this little Lamb
Had carefully prepared to Slam,
And Down it came! It knocked her flat!

It laid her out! She looked
like that.

* * *

Her funeral Sermon (which was long
And followed by a Sacred Song)
Mentioned her Virtues, it is true,
But dwelt upon her Vices too,

And showed the Dreadful End of One
Who goes and slams the door for Fun.

*   *   *

The children who were brought to hear
The awful Tale from far and near
Were much impressed, and inly swore
They never more would slam the Door.
– As often they had done before.

George,

Who played with a Dangerous Toy, and suffered a Catastrophe of considerable Dimensions.

When George's Grandmamma was told

That George had been as good as Gold,
She Promised in the Afternoon
To buy him an *Immense BALLOON.*

And so she did; but when it came,
It got into the candle flame,
And being of a dangerous sort
Exploded

with a loud report!

The Lights went out! The Windows broke!
The Room was filled with reeking smoke.
And in the darkness shrieks and yells
Were mingled with Electric Bells,
And falling masonry and groans,
And crunching, as of broken bones,
And dreadful shrieks, when, worst of all,
The House itself began to fall!
It tottered, shuddered to and fro,
Then crashed into the street below –
Which happened to be Savile Row.

*　*　*

When Help arrived, among the Dead

Were　　　　　Cousin Mary,

Little Fred,

66

The Footmen

(both of them),

The Groom,

The man that cleaned the Billiard-Room,

The Chaplain, and

        The Still-Room Maid.
And I am dreadfully afraid
That Monsieur Champignon, the Chef,
Will now be

        permanently deaf –

And both his Aides

are much the same;
While George, who was in part to blame,
Received, you will regret to hear,
A nasty lump

behind the ear.

MORAL

The moral is that little Boys
Should not be given dangerous Toys.

Charles Augustus Fortescue,

Who always Did what was Right, and so accumulated an

Immense Fortune.

The nicest child I ever knew
Was Charles Augustus Fortescue.
He never lost his cap, or tore
His stockings or his pinafore:
In eating Bread he made no Crumbs,
He was extremely fond
    of sums,

To which, however,
   he preferred
The Parsing of a
   Latin Word –
He sought, when it
   was in his power,
For information twice an hour,

And as for finding Mutton-Fat
Unappetising, far from that!
He often, at his Father's Board,
Would beg them, of his own accord,

To give him, if they did not mind,
The Greasiest Morsels they could find –
His Later Years did not belie
The Promise of his Infancy.

In Public Life he always tried
To take a judgment Broad and Wide;

In Private, none was more than he
Renowed for quiet courtesy.
He rose at once in his Career,
And long before his Fortieth Year
Had wedded

Fifi, Only Child
Of Bunyan, First Lord Aberfylde.
He thus became immensely Rich,
And built the Splendid Mansion which
Is called

73

"The Cedars,
Muswell Hill,"

Where he resides in Affluence still,
To show what Everybody might
Become by

SIMPLY DOING RIGHT.

NEW
CAUTIONARY TALES

Illustrated by Quentin Blake

A Reproof of Gluttony

The Elephant will eat of hay
Some four and twenty tons a day,
And in his little eyes express
His unaffected thankfulness

That Providence should deign to find
Him food of this delicious kind.
While they that pay for all the hay
Will frequently be heard to say
How highly privileged they feel
To help him make so large a meal.

The Boa Constrictor dotes on goats;
The Horse is quite content with oats,
Or will alternatively pass
A happy morning munching grass.

The great Ant Eater of Taluz
Consumes – or people say he does –
Not only what his name implies
But even ordinary flies:
And Marmosets and Chimpanzees
Are happy on the nuts of trees.

The Lion from the burning slopes
Of Atlas lives on Antelopes,
And only adds the flesh of men

By way of relish now and then;

As Cheetahs – yes, and Tigers, too,
And Jaguars of the Andes – do.
The Lobster, I have heard it said,
Eats nobody till he is dead;

And Cobras, though they have the sense
To poison you in self-defence,
Restrict their food to birds and hares:
Which also may be true of Bears.
Indeed wherever we survey
Our Humble Friends we find that they
Confine their appetites to what
May happen to be on the spot.

Simplicity and moderation
Distinguish all the Brute Creation.
But Man – proud man! (as Dryden sings)
Though wolfing quantities of things –
Smoked Salmon in transparent slices,
And Turbot à la Reine,

and Ices,

And Truffled Pies and Caviare,
And Chinese Ginger from the Jar;
And Oysters;

and a kind of stuff
Called Cassouletto (good enough!)

And Mutton duly steeped in claret
(Or jumped with young shallot and carrot),
And Chicken Livers done with rice,
And Quails (which, I am told are Mice),
And Peaches from a sunny wall,
And – Lord! I don't know what and all! –
Oh! Yes! And Sausages

– is not
Contented with his Prandial lot.

MORAL

The Moral is (I think, at least)
That Man is an UNGRATEFUL BEAST.

Maria

Who made Faces and a Deplorable Marriage

Maria loved to pull a face:
And no such commonplace grimace
As you or I or anyone
Might make at grandmamma for fun.
But one where nose and mouth and all

Were screwed into a kind of ball,
The which – as you may well expect –
Produced a horrible effect
On those it was directed at.

One morning she was struck like that! –
Her features took their final mould
In shapes that made your blood run cold
And wholly lost their former charm.

Mamma, in agonised alarm,
Consulted a renowned Masseuse
– An old and valued friend of hers –

Who rubbed the wretched child for days
In five and twenty different ways
And after that began again.

But all in vain! – But all in vain!

The years advance: Maria grows
Into a Blooming English Rose –
With every talent, every grace
(Save in this trifle of the face).
She sang, recited, laughed and played
At all that an accomplished maid
Should play with skill to be of note –
Golf, the Piano, and the Goat;
She talked in French till all was blue
And knew a little German too.
She told the tales that soldiers tell,

She also danced extremely well,

Her wit was pointed, loud and raw,
She shone at laying down the law,
She drank liqueurs instead of tea,

Her verse was admirably free
And quoted in the latest books –
But people couldn't stand her looks.

Her parents had with thoughtful care
Proclaimed her genius everywhere,
Nor quite concealed a wealth which sounds
Enormous – thirty million pounds –

And further whispered it that she
Could deal with it exclusively.

They did not hide her chief defect,
But what with birth and intellect
And breeding and such ample means,
And still in her delightful 'teens,
A girl like our Maria (they thought)
Should make the kind of match she ought.
Those who had seen her here at home
Might hesitate: but Paris? Rome? . . .
– The foreigners should take the bait.

And so they did. At any rate,
The greatest men of every land

Arrived in shoals to seek her hand,
Grand Dukes, Commanders of the Fleece,
Mysterious Millionaires from Greece,
And exiled Kings in large amounts,

Ambassadors and Papal Counts,
And Rastaqouères from Palamerez
And Famous Foreign Secretairies,

They came along in turns to call
But *all* – without exception, *all* –
Though with determination set,
Yet, when they actually *met*,

Would start convulsively as though
They had received a sudden blow,

And mumbling a discreet good-day
Would shuffle, turn and slink away.

The upshot of it was Maria
Was married to a neighbouring Squire
Who, being blind, could never guess
His wife's appalling ugliness.

The man was independent, dull,
Offensive, poor and masterful.
It was a very dreadful thing! . . .

Now let us turn to Sarah Byng.

Sarah Byng

Who could not read and was tossed into

a thorny hedge by a bull

Some years ago you heard me sing
My doubts on Alexander Byng.
His sister Sarah now inspires
My jaded Muse, my failing fires.
Of Sarah Byng the tale is told
How when the child was twelve years old
She could not read or write a line.

Her sister Jane, though barely nine,
Could spout the Catechism through

And parts of Matthew Arnold too,

While little Bill
who came between

Was quite unnaturally keen
On
"Athalie," by Jean Racine.

But not so Sarah! Not so Sal!
She was a most uncultured girl
Who didn't care a pinch of snuff
For any literary stuff
And gave the classics all a miss.
Observe the consequence of this!
As she was walking home one day,
Upon the fields across her way
A gate, securely padlocked, stood,
And by its side a piece of wood
On which was painted plain and full,

BEWARE THE VERY
FURIOUS BULL.
Alas!
    The young illiterate
Went blindly forward
    to her fate,
And ignorantly climbed
    the gate!

Now happily the Bull that day
Was rather in the mood for play
Than goring people through and through
As Bulls so very often do:

He tossed her lightly with his horns
Into a prickly hedge of thorns,

And stood by laughing while she strode
And pushed and struggled to the road.

The lesson was not lost upon
The child, who since has always gone
A long way round to keep away
From signs, whatever they may say,
And leaves a padlocked gate alone.
Moreover she has wisely grown
Confirmed in her instinctive guess
      That literature breeds distress.

Jack and his Pony, Tom

Jack had a little pony – Tom;

He frequently would take it from
The stable where it used to stand
And give it sugar with his hand.
He also gave it oats and hay
And carrots

twenty times a day
And grass in basketfuls, and greens,

And swedes and mangolds

                              also beans
And patent foods from various sources

And bread (which isn't good for horses)
And chocolate and apple-rings

And lots and lots of other things
The most of which do not agree
With Polo Ponies such as he.
And all in such a quantity
As ruined his digestion wholly
And turned him from a Ponopoly
– I mean a Polo Pony – into
A case that clearly must be seen to.
Because he swelled and swelled and swelled.
Which, when the kindly boy beheld,
He gave him medicine by the pail
And malted milk, and nutmeg ale,

And yet it only swelled the more
Until its stomach touched the floor,

And then it heaved and groaned as well
And staggered, till at last it fell

And found it could not rise again.
Jack wept and prayed – but all in vain.
The pony died and as it died
Kicked him severely in the side.

MORAL
Kindness to animals should be
Attuned to their brutality.

Tom and his Pony, Jack

Tom had a little pony – Jack:

He vaulted lightly on its back
And galloped off for miles and miles,
A-leaping hedges, gates and stiles,

And shouting "Yoicks!" and "Tally-Ho!"
And "Heads I win!" and "Tails below!"

And many another sporting phrase.
He rode like this for several days,
Until the pony, feeling tired,
Collapsed, looked heavenward and expired.

His father made a fearful row.
He said "By Gum, you've done it now!
Here lies – a carcase on the ground –
No less than five and twenty pound!

Indeed the value of the beast
Would probably have much increased.
His teeth were false; and all were told
That he was only four years old.
Oh! Curse it all! I tell you plain
I'll never let you ride again."

MORAL

His father died when he was twenty
And left three horses, which is plenty.

About John,

Who lost a fortune by Throwing Stones

JOHN VAVASSOUR
DE QUENTIN JONES

Was very fond of throwing stones

At Horses, People, Passing Trains,
But 'specially at Windowpanes.

Like many of the Upper
Class
He liked the
Sound of
Broken
Glass*

It bucked him up and made him gay:
It was his favourite form of Play.
But the Amusement cost him dear,
My children, as you now shall hear.

*A line I stole with
subtle daring
From Wing-Commander
Maurice Baring

JOHN VAVASSOUR DE QUENTIN had
An uncle, who adored the lad:

And often chuckled; "Wait until
You see what's left you in my will!"

Nor were the words without import,
Because this uncle did a sort
Of something in the City, which
Had made him fabulously rich.
(Although his brother, John's papa,
Was poor, as many fathers are.)

He had a lot of stocks and shares
And half a street in Buenos Aires*
A bank in Rio, and a line
Of Steamers to the Argentine.
And options more than I can tell,
And bits of Canada as well;
He even had a mortgage on
The House inhabited by John.
His will, the cause of all the fuss,
Was carefully indited thus:

"This is the last and solemn Will
Of Uncle William – known as Bill.

*But this pronunciation varies.
Some people call it Bu-enos Airés.

I do bequeath, devise and give
By Execution Mandative
The whole amount of what I've got
(It comes to a tremendous lot!)
In seizin to devolve upon
My well-beloved nephew John.
(And here the witnesses will sign
Their names upon the dotted line.)"

Such was the Legal Instrument
Expressing Uncle Bill's intent.

As time went on declining Health
Transmogrified this Man of Wealth;
And it was excellently clear
That Uncle Bill's demise was near.

    At last his sole idea of fun
    Was sitting snoozling in the sun

So once, when he would
   take the air,
They wheeled him in his
   Patent Chair

(By "They," I mean his Nurse, who came
From Dorchester upon the Thame:
Miss Charming was the Nurse's name).
To where beside a little wood
A long abandoned green-house stood,
And there he sank into a doze
Of senile and inept repose.
But not for long his drowsy ease!
A stone came whizzing through the trees,
And caught him smartly in the eye.
He woke with an appalling cry,
And shrieked in agonizing tones:
"Oh! Lord! Whoever's throwing stones!"

Miss Charming,
who was standing near,
Said: "That was
Master John, I fear!"

"Go, get my Ink-pot and my Quill,
My Blotter and my Famous Will."
Miss Charming flew as though on wings
To fetch these necessary things,
And Uncle William ran his pen
Through "well-beloved John," and then
Proceeded, in the place of same,
To substitute Miss Charming's name:

Who now resides in Portman Square
And is accepted everywhere.

Peter Goole

Who Ruined his Father and Mother by Extravagance

PART I

Young Peter Goole, a child of nine
Gave little reason to complain.

Though an imaginative youth
He very often told the truth,
And never tried to black the eyes
Of Comrades of superior size.

He did his lessons (more or less)
Without extravagant distress,
And showed sufficient intellect,
But failed in one severe defect;
It seems he wholly lacked a sense
Of limiting the day's expense,

And money ran between his hands
Like water through the Ocean Sands.
Such conduct could not but affect
His parent's fortune, which was wrecked
Like many and many another one
By folly in a spendthrift son:
By that most tragical mischance,
An Only Child's Extravagance.

There came a day when Mr. Goole
– The Father of this little fool –
With nothing in the bank at all
Was up against it, like a wall.

He wrang his hands, exclaiming, "If
I only had a bit of Stiff
How different would be my life!"
Whereat his true and noble wife
Replied, to comfort him, "Alas!
I said that this would come to pass!
Nothing can keep us off the rocks
But Peter's little Money Box."

The Father, therefore (and his wife),
They prised it open with a knife —

But nothing could be found therein
Save two bone buttons and a pin.

129

PART II

They had to sell the house and grounds
For less than twenty thousand pounds,
And so retired, with broken hearts,
To vegetate in foreign parts,

And ended their declining years
At Blidah – which is near Algiers.

There in the course of time
                       they died,
   And there lie buried
              side by side.

While when we turn to Peter, he
The cause of this catastrophe,
There fell upon him such a fate
As makes me shudder to relate.
Just in its fifth and final year,
His University Career
Was blasted by the new and dread
Necessity of earning bread.
He was compelled to join a firm
Of Brokers – in the summer term!
And even now, at twenty-five,
He has to
　　　　　W O R K
　　　　　　　　　to keep alive!

Yes! All day long from 10 till 4!
For half the year or even more;

With but an hour or two to spend
At luncheon with a city friend.

Aunt Jane

"Mamma" said AMANDA "I want to know what
    Our relatives mean when they say
That Aunt Jane is a Gorgon who ought to be shot,
    Or at any rate taken away.

"Pray what is a Gorgon and why do you shoot
    It? Or are its advances refused?
Or is it perhaps a maleficent Brute?
    I protest I am wholly bemused."

"The Term," said her Mother, "is certain to pain,
    And is quite inexcusably rude.
Moveover Aunt Jane, though uncommonly plain,
    Is also uncommonly good.

"She provides information without hesitation,
    For people unwilling to learn;
And often bestows good advice
                                        upon those
Who give her no thanks in return.

"She is down before anyone's up in the place –
That is, up before anyone's down.

Her Domestics are awed by the shape of her face
And they tremble with fear at her frown.

"Her visiting list is of Clergymen who
Have reached a respectable age,

And she pays her companion
                    MISS ANGELA DREW
A sufficient and regular wage.

"Her fortune is large, though we often remark
    On a modesty rare in the rich;
For her nearest and dearest are quite in the dark
    As to what she will leave, or to which.

"Her conduct has ever been totally free
    From censorious whispers of ill,
At any rate, since 1903 –
    And probably earlier still.

"Your Father's dear sister presents in a word,
    A model for all of her sex,
With a firmness of will that is never deterred,
    And a confidence nothing can vex.

"I can only desire that you too should aspire
    To such earthly reward as appears
In a high reputation, at present entire,
    After Heaven knows how many years.

"So in future remember to turn a deaf ear
    To detraction – and now run away
To your brothers and sisters whose laughter I hear
    In the garden below us at play."

"Oh, thank you, Mamma!"
            said AMANDA at that,
                And ran off to the innocent band

Who were merrily burying Thomas the Cat
Right up to his neck in the sand.

On Food

Alas! What various tastes in food,
Divide the human brotherhood!

Birds in their little nests agree
  With Chinamen, but not with me.
Colonials like their oysters hot,
Their omelettes heavy – I do not.
The French are
    fond of slugs
      and frogs,

The Siamese eat puppy-dogs.

The nobles at the brilliant Court
Of Muscovy, consumed a sort
Of candles held and eaten
                    thus

As though they were asparagus.

The Spaniard, I have heard it said,
Eats garlic, by itself, on bread:

Now just suppose a friend or dun
Dropped in to lunch at half-past one
And you were jovially to say,

"Here's bread and garlic! Peg away!"
I doubt if you would gain your end
Or soothe the dun, or please the friend.

In Italy the traveller notes
With great disgust the flesh of goats
Appearing on the table d'hôtes;

And even this the natives spoil
By frying it in rancid oil.

In Maryland they charge like sin
For nasty stuff called terrapin;
And when they ask you out to dine
At Washington, instead of wine,
They give you water from the spring

With lumps of ice for flavouring,
That sometimes kill and always freeze
The high plenipotentiaries.

146

In Massachusetts all the way
From Boston down to Buzzards Bay
They feed you till you want to die
On rhubarb pie and pumpkin pie,
And horrible huckleberry pie,
And when you summon the strength to cry,
"What is there else that I can try?"
They stare at you in mild surprise
And serve you other kinds of pies.

And I with these mine eyes have seen
A dreadful stuff called Margarine
Consumed by men in Bethnal Green.
But I myself that here complain
Confess restriction quite in vain.
I feel my native courage fail
To see a Gascon eat a snail;

I dare not ask abroad for tea;
No cannibal can dine with me;

And all the world is torn and rent
By varying views on nutriment.
And yet upon the other hand,
De gustibus non disputand –

                – *Um.*

THE
BAD CHILD'S
BOOK OF BEASTS

Illustrated by B.T.B

INTRODUCTION

I CALL you bad, my little child,
    Upon the title page,
Because a manner rude and wild
    Is common at your age.

The Moral of this priceless work
    (If rightly understood)
Will make you – from a little Turk –
    Unnaturally good.

Do not as evil children do,
    Who on the slightest grounds
Will imitate the Kangaroo,
With wild unmeaning bounds:

Do not as children badly bred,
    Who eat like little Hogs,
And when they have to go to bed
    Will whine like Puppy Dogs:

Who take their manners from the Ape,
    Their habits from the Bear,
Indulge the loud unseemly jape,
    And never brush their hair.

But so control your actions that
Your friends may all repeat,

"This child is dainty as the Cat,
And as the Owl discreet."

The Yak

As a friend to the children

commend me the Yak.

You will find it exactly the thing:
It will carry and fetch,

you can ride on its back,

Or lead it about with a string.

The Tartar who dwells on the plains of Thibet
(A desolate region of snow)

Has for centuries made it a nursery pet,
And surely the Tartar should know!

Then tell your papa where the Yak can be got,

And if he is awfully rich
He will buy you the creature —

or else he will *not*.

(I cannot be positive which.)

The Polar Bear

The Polar Bear is unaware
    Of cold that cuts me through:
For why? He has a coat of hair.
    I wish I had one too!

The Lion

The Lion, the Lion, he dwells in the waste,
He has a big head and a very small waist;

But his shoulders are stark, and his jaws they
   are grim,
And a good little child will not play with him.

The Tiger

The Tiger on the other hand,

is kittenish and mild,
He makes a pretty playfellow for any little child;
And mothers of large families (who claim to
common sense)

Will find a Tiger well repays the trouble and
expense.

The Dromedary

The Dromedary is a cheerful bird:

I cannot say the same about the Kurd.

The Whale

The Whale that wanders round the Pole

Is not a table fish.

You cannot bake or boil him whole
Nor serve him in a dish;

But you may cut his blubber up
And melt it down for oil.

And so replace the colza bean
(A product of the soil).

These facts should all be noted down
    And ruminated on,

By every boy in Oxford town
    Who wants to be a Don.

The Camel

"The Ship of the Desert"

The Hippopotamus

I shoot the Hippopotamus

with bullets made of platinum,

Because if I use leaden ones

his hide is sure to flatten 'em.

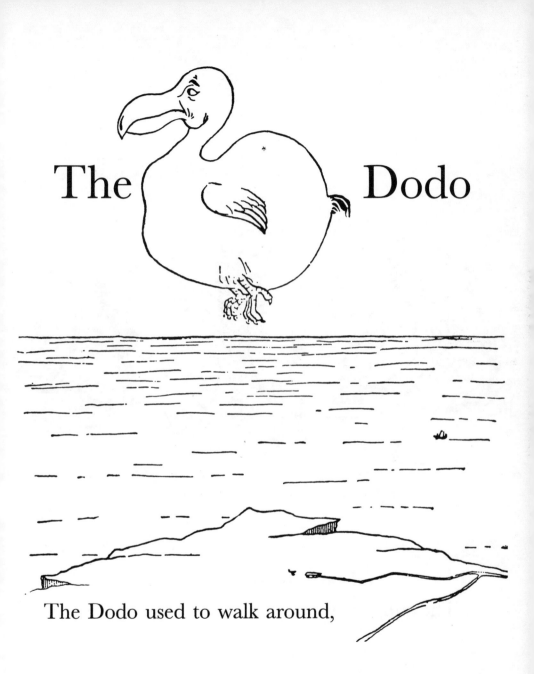

The Dodo

The Dodo used to walk around,

And take the sun and air.
The sun yet warms his native ground –

The Dodo is not there!

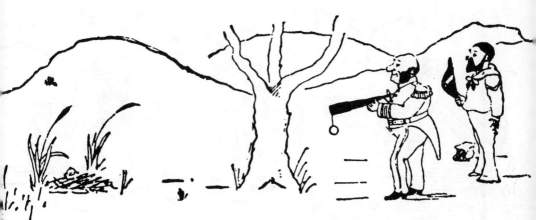

The voice which used to squawk and squeak
Is now for ever dumb –

Yet may you see his bones and beak
All in the Mu-se-um.

The Marmozet

The species Man and Marmozet
  Are intimately linked;

The Marmozet survives as yet,
  But Men are all extinct.

The Camelopard

The Camelopard it is said
    By travellers (who never lie),
He cannot stretch out straight in bed
    Because he is so high.

The clouds surround his lofty head,
    His hornlets touch the sky.
How shall I hunt this quadruped?
    I cannot tell! Not I!

(A picture of how people try
And fail to hit that head so high.)

I'll buy a little parachute
(A common parachute with wings),
I'll fill it full of arrowroot
And other necessary things,

And I will slay this fearful brute
With stones and sticks and guns and slings.

(A picture of how people shoot
With comfort from a parachute.)

The Learned Fish

This learned Fish has not sufficient brains
To go into the water when it rains.

The Elephant

When people call this beast to mind,

They marvel more and more
At such a

LITTLE tail behind,

So *LARGE* a trunk before.

The Big Baboon

The Big Baboon is found upon
The plains of Cariboo:

He goes about with nothing on

(A shocking thing to do).

But if he dressed respectably
And let his whiskers grow,

How like this Big Baboon would be

To Mister So-and so!

The Rhinoceros

Rhinoceros, your hide looks all undone,

You do not take my fancy in the least:

You have a horn where other brutes have none:
Rhinoceros, you are an ugly beast.

The Frog

Be kind and tender to the Frog,
　　And do not call him names,

As "Slimy skin," or "Polly-wog"
    Or likewise "Ugly James,"
Or "Gap-a-grin," or "Toad-gone-wrong,"
    Or "Bill, Bandy-knees":

The Frog is justly sensitive
    To epithets like these.

No animal will more repay
    A treatment kind and fair;
At least so lonely people say
    Who keep a frog (and, by the way,
They are extremely rare).

Oh! My!

MORE BEASTS
FOR WORSE
CHILDREN

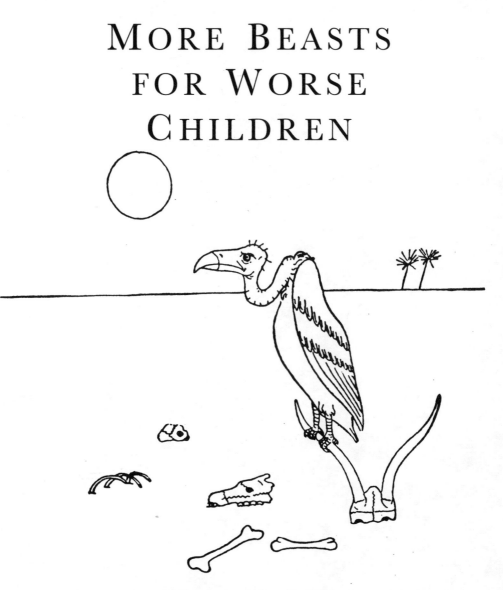

Illustrated by B.T.B

DEDICATION

To
Miss ALICE WOLCOTT BRINLEY,
of Philadelphia

INTRODUCTION

The parents of the learned child
    (His father and his mother)
Were utterly aghast to note
The facts he would at random quote
On creatures curious, rare and wild;
    And wondering, asked each other:

"An idle little child like this,
     How is it that he knows
What years of close analysis
     Are powerful to disclose?

Our brains are trained, our books are big
     And yet we always fail

To answer why the Guinea-pig
Is born without a tail.

Or why the Wanderoo* should rant
In wild, unmeaning rhymes,

*Sometimes called the "Lion-tailed or tufted Baboon of Ceylon."

Whereas the Indian Elephant
Will only read *The Times*.

Perhaps he found a way to slip
    Unnoticed to the Zoo,
And gave the Pachyderm a tip,
    Or pumped the Wanderoo.

Or even by an artful plan
    Deceived our watchful eyes,
And interviewed the Pelican,
    Who is extremely wise."

"Oh! no," said he, in humble tone,
  With shy but conscious look,
"Such facts I never could have known
  But for this little book."

The Python

A PYTHON I should not advise, –
It needs a doctor for its eyes,
And has the measles yearly.

However, if you feel inclined
To get one (to improve your mind,
And not from fashion merely),
Allow no music near its cage;

And when it flies into a rage
Chastise it, most severely.

I had an aunt in Yucatan
Who bought a Python from a man
    And kept it for a pet.
She died, because she never knew
These simple little rules and few; –

The Snake is living yet.

The Welsh Mutton

The Cambrian Welsh or Mountain Sheep
    Is of the Ovine race,
His conversation is not deep,
    But then – observe his face!

The Porcupine

What! would you slap the Porcupine?
    Unhappy child – desist!
Alas! that any friend of mine
    Should turn Tupto-philist.*

---

* From $\tau\upsilon\pi\tau\omega$ = I strike; $\phi\iota\lambda\acute{\epsilon}\omega$ = I love; one that loves to strike. The word is not found in classical Greek, nor does it occur among the writers of the Renaissance – nor anywhere else.

To strike the meanest and the least
  Of creatures is a sin,

How much more bad to beat a beast
With prickles on its skin.

The Scorpion

The Scorpion is as black as soot,
    He dearly loves to bite;
He is a most unpleasant brute
    To find in bed, at night.

The Crocodile

Whatever our faults, we can always engage
That no fancy or fable shall sully our page,
    So take note of what follows, I beg.
This creature so grand and august in its age,
    In its youth is hatched out of an egg.

And oft in some far Coptic town
The Missionary sits him down
    To breakfast by the Nile:
The heart beneath his priestly gown
    Is innocent of guile;

When suddenly the rigid frown
Of Panic is observed to drown
   His customary smile.

Why does he start and leap amain,

And scour the sandy Libyan plain

Like one that wants to catch a train,

Or wrestles with internal pain?

Because he finds his egg contain –
Green, hungry, horrible and plain –
　An Infant Crocodile.

The Vulture

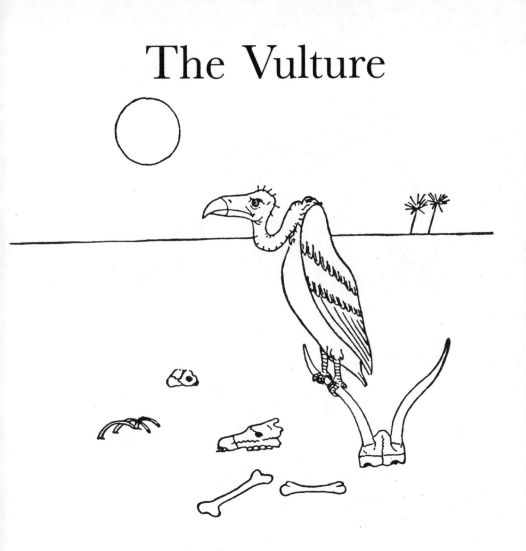

The Vulture eats between his meals,
And that's the reason why

He very, very rarely feels
    As well as you and I.
His eye is dull, his head is bald,
    His neck is growing thinner.
Oh! what a lesson for us all
    To only eat at dinner!

The Bison

The Bison is vain, and (I write it with pain)
The Door-mat you see on his head

Is not, as some learned professors maintain,
The opulent growth of a genius' brain;

But is sewn on with needle and thread.

The Viper

Yet another great truth I record in my verse,
That some Vipers are venomous, some the

reverse;

A fact you may prove if you try,
By procuring two Vipers, and letting them bite;

With the *first* you are only the worse for a fright,

But after the *second* you die.

The Llama

The Llama is a woolly sort of fleecy hairy goat,
With an indolent expression and an undulating
                                              throat
Like an unsuccessful literary man.

And I know the place he lives in (or at least –
I think I do)
It is Ecuador, Brazil or Chile – possibly Peru;
You must find it in the Atlas if you can.

The Llama of the Pampasses you never should
confound
(In spite of a deceptive similarity of sound)
With the Lhama who is Lord of Turkestan.

For the former is a beautiful and valuable beast,
But the latter is not lovable nor useful in the least;
And the Ruminant is preferable surely to the Priest
Who battens on the woeful superstitions of the East,
    The Mongol of the Monastery of Shan.

The Chamois

The Chamois inhabits
Lucerne, where his habits
   (Though why I have not an idea-r)
Give him sudden short spasms
On the brink of deep chasms,
   And he lives in perpetual fear.

The Frozen Mammoth

This Creature, though rare, is still found to the
East

Of the Northern Siberian Zone.

It is known to the whole of that primitive group
That the carcass will furnish an excellent soup,
Though the cooking it offers one drawback

                                 at least
(Of a serious nature I own):

If the skin be *but punctured* before it is boiled,
Your confection is wholly and utterly spoiled.

And hence (on account of the size of the beast)
The dainty is nearly unknown.

The Microbe

The Microbe is so very small
You cannot make him out at all,
But many sanguine people hope
To see him through a microscope.
His jointed tongue that lies beneath
A hundred curious rows of teeth;
His seven tufted tails with lots
Of lovely pink and purple spots,

On each of which a pattern stands,
Composed of forty separate bands;
His eyebrows of a tender green;
All these have never yet been seen –
But Scientists, who ought to know,
Assure us that they must be so . . .
Oh! let us never, never doubt
What nobody is sure about!

MORE PEERS

Verses by H. BELLOC

Pictures by B. T. B.

Lord Roehampton

During a late election Lord
Roehampton strained a vocal chord
From shouting, very loud and high,
To lots and lots of people why
The Budget in his own opin-
-Ion should not be allowed to win.

He sought a Specialist, who said:

"You have a swelling in the head:
Your Larynx is a thought relaxed
And you are greatly over-taxed."

"I am indeed! On every side!"
The Earl (for such he was) replied

In hoarse excitement . . . "Oh! My Lord,
You jeopardize your vocal chord!"
Broke in the worthy Specialist.
"Come! Here's the treatment! I insist!
To Bed! to Bed! And do not speak
A single word till Wednesday week,
When I will come and set you free
(If you are cured) and take my fee."

On Wednesday week the Doctor hires
A Brand-new Car with Brand-new Tyres
And Brand-new Chauffeur all complete
For visiting South Audley Street.

* * *

But what is this? No Union Jack
Floats on the Stables at the back!
No Toffs escorting Ladies fair
Perambulate the Gay Parterre.
A 'Scutcheon hanging lozenge-wise
And draped in crape appals his eyes
Upon the mansion's ample door,
To which he wades through
      heaps of Straw,[†]

† This is the first and only time
That I have used this sort of Rhyme.

252

And which a Butler, drowned in tears,
On opening but confirms his fears:
"Oh! Sir! – Prepare to hear the worst! . . .
Last night my kind old master burst.
And what is more, I doubt if he
Has left enough to pay your fee.
The Budget—"

With a dreadful oath,
The Specialist, denouncing both
The Budget *and* the House of Lords,
Buzzed angrily Bayswaterwards.

* * *

And ever since, as I am told,
Gets it beforehand; and in gold.

Lord Calvin

Lord Calvin thought the Bishops should not sit
As Peers of Parliament. And *argued* it!

In spite of which, for years, and years, and years,
They went on sitting with their fellow-peers.

Lord Henry Chase

What happened to Lord Henry Chase?
He got into a Libel Case!

The Daily Howl had said that he –
But could not prove it perfectly

To Judge or Jury's satisfaction:
His Lordship, therefore, won the action.

But, as the damages were small

He gave them to a Hospital.

Lord Heygate

LORD HEYGATE had a troubled face
His furniture was commonplace –
The sort of Peer who well might pass
For someone of the middle class.
I do not think you want to hear
About this unimportant Peer,
So let us leave him to discourse
About LORD EPSOM and his horse.

Lord Epsom

A Horse, Lord Epsom did bestride
With mastery and quiet pride.
He dug his spurs into its hide.

The Horse, discerning it was pricked,

Incontinently bucked and kicked,
A thing that no one could predict!

Lord Epsom clearly understood
The High-bred creature's nervous mood,
As only such a horseman could.

Dismounting,

he was heard to say
That it was kinder to delay
His pleasure to a future day.

* * *

He had the Hunter led away.

Lord Finchley

Lord Finchley tried to mend the Electric Light
Himself.

It struck him dead: And serve him right!
It is the business of the wealthy man
To give employment to the artisan.

Lord Ali-Baba

Lord Ali-Baba was a Turk
Who hated every kind of work,
And would repose for hours at ease
With Houris seated on his knees.

A happy life! – Until, one day

Mossoo Alphonse Effendi Bey
(A Younger Turk: the very cream
And essence of the New Régime)
Dispelled this Oriental dream
By granting him a place at Court,

High Coffee-grinder to the Porte,
Unpaid: –

In which exalted Post
His Lordship yielded up the ghost.

Lord Hippo

Lord Hippo suffered fearful loss
By putting money on a horse
Which he believed, if it were pressed,
Would run far faster than the rest:

For someone who was in the know
Had confidently told him so.

But on the morning of the race

It only took

the *seventh* place!

Picture the Viscount's great surprise!
He scarcely could believe his eyes!

He sought the Individual who
Had laid him odds at 9 to 2,
Suggesting as a useful tip
That they should enter Partnership
And put to joint account the debt
Arising from his foolish bet.

But when the Bookie – oh! my word,
I only wish you could have heard
The way he roared he did not think,
And hoped that they might strike him pink!

Lord Hippo simply turned and ran
From this infuriated man.
Despairing, maddened and distraught
He utterly collapsed and sought
His sire, the Earl of Potamus,

And brokenly addressed him thus:
"Dread Sire – to-day at Ascot – I . . ."
His genial parent made reply:
"Come! Come! Come! Come! Don't look
                              so glum!
Trust your Papa and name the sum . . .

WHAT?

       . . . *Fifteen hundred thousand?* . . . Hum!
However . . . stiffen up, you wreck;
Boys will be boys – so here's the cheque!"
Lord Hippo, feeling deeply – well,
More grateful than he cared to tell –
Punted the lot on Little Nell: –

And got a telegram at dinner

To say that he had backed the Winner!

Lord Uncle Tom

Lord Uncle Tom was different from
    What other nobles are.
For they are yellow or pink, I think,
    But he was   black as tar.

He had his father's debonair
　　And rather easy pride:
But his complexion and his hair

Were from the mother's side.

He often mingled in debate
    And latterly displayed
Experience of peculiar weight
    Upon the Cocoa-trade.

But now he speaks no more.
    The BILL Which he could not abide,
It preyed upon his mind until
    He sickened, paled, and died.

Lord Lucky

Lord Lucky, by a curious fluke,
Became a most important duke.
From living in a vile Hotel

A long way east of Camberwell

He rose in less than half an hour
To riches, dignity and power.
It happened in the following way: –
The Real Duke went out one day
To shoot with several people, one

Of whom had never used a gun.
This gentleman (a Mr. Meyer
Of Rabley Abbey, Rutlandshire),
As he was scrambling through the brake,

Discharged his weapon by mistake,
And plugged about an ounce of lead
Piff-bang into his Grace's Head –
Who naturally fell down dead.

His heir, Lord Ugly, roared, "You Brute!
Take that to teach you how to shoot!"

Whereat he volleyed left and right;
But being somewhat short of sight,
His right-hand Barrel only got
The second heir, Lord Poddleplot;

The while the left-hand charge (or choke)
Accounted for another bloke,
Who stood with an astounded air
Bewildered by the whole affair
– And was the third remaining heir.

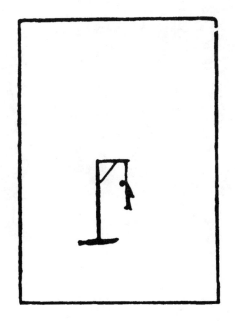

After the Execution (which
Is something rare among the Rich)

Lord Lucky, while of course, he needed
Some help to prove his claim,

succeeded.

– But after his succession, though
All this was over years ago,
He only once indulged the whim
Of asking Meyer to lunch with him.

Lord Canton

The reason that the present Lord Canton
Succeeded lately to his Brother John
Was that his Brother John, the elder son,
Died rather suddenly at forty-one.

The insolence of an Italian guide

Appears to be the reason that he died.

Lord Abbott

Lord Abbott's coronet was far too small,
So small, that as he sauntered down Whitehall
Even the youthful Proletariat
(Who probably mistook it for a Hat)
Remarked on its exiguous extent.

Here is a picture of the incident.

A
MORAL
ALPHABET

Illustrated by B.T.B

stands for

Archibald who told no lies,
And got this lovely volume for a prize.

The Upper School had combed and oiled
                                               their hair,
And all the Parents of the Boys were there.
In words that ring like thunder through the
                                                 Hall,
Draw tears from some and loud applause
                                                 from all,

The Pedagogue, with Pardonable Joy,
Bestows the Gift upon the Radiant Boy: –

"Accept the Noblest Work produced as yet"
(Says he) "upon the English Alphabet;
"Next term I shall examine you, to find
"If you have read it thoroughly. So mind!"

And while the Boys and Parents cheered so loud,
That out of doors

a large and anxious crowd
Had gathered and was blocking up the street,
The admirable child resumed his seat.

MORAL
Learn from this justly irritating Youth,
To brush your Hair and Teeth and tell the Truth.

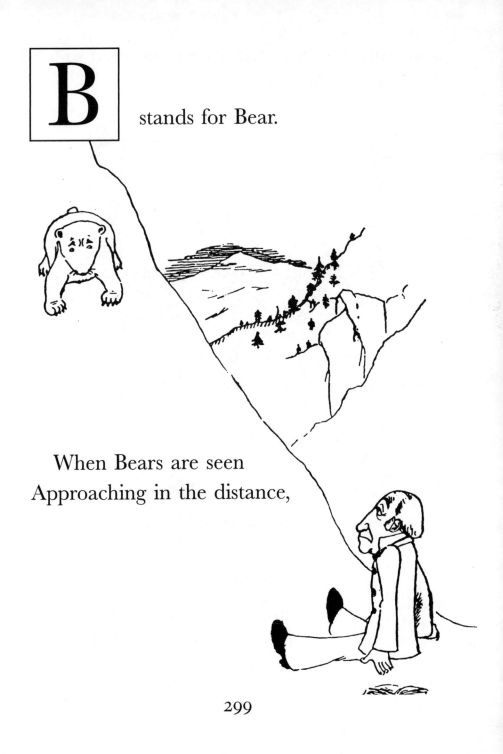

B
stands for Bear.

When Bears are seen
Approaching in the distance,

Make up your mind at once between
Retreat and Armed Resistance.

A Gentleman remained to fight –
With what result for him?

The Bear, with ill-concealed delight,
  Devoured him, Limb by Limb.

Another Person turned and ran;
  He ran extremely hard:
The Bear was faster than the Man,
  And beat him by a yard.

MORAL

Decisive action in the hour of need
Denotes the Hero, but does not succeed.

C stands for Cobra;
       when the Cobra bites

An Indian Judge, the Judge spends restless nights.

MORAL

This creature, though disgusting and appalling,
Conveys no kind of Moral worth recalling.

D

The Dreadful Dinotherium he
Will have to do his best for D.
The early world observed with awe
His back, indented like a saw.
His look was gay, his voice was strong;
His tail was neither short nor long;

His trunk, or elongated nose,
Was not so large as some suppose;
His teeth, as all the world allows,
Were graminivorous, like a cow's.

He therefore should have wished to pass
Long peaceful nights upon the Grass,
But being mad the brute preferred
To roost in branches, like a bird.*
A creature heavier than a whale,
You see at once, could hardly fail
To suffer badly when he slid.

* We have good reason to suppose
He did so, from his claw-like toes.

And tumbled

(as he always did).
His fossil, therefore, comes to light
All broken up: and serve him right.

MORAL

If you were born to walk the ground,
Remain there; do not fool around.

E stands for Egg

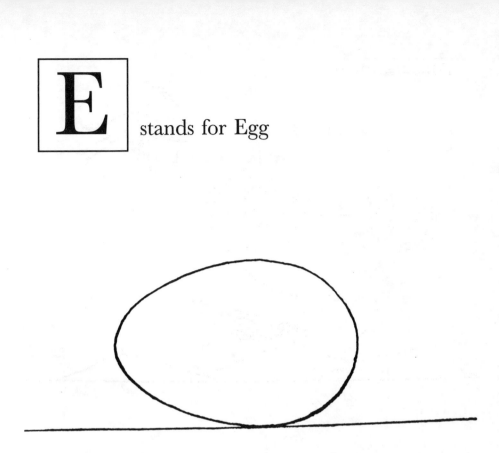

MORAL
The Moral of this verse
Is applicable to the Young. Be terse.

F

for a Family
taking a walk

In Arcadia Terrace, no doubt:
The parents indulge in intelligent talk,
   While the children they gambol about.

At a quarter-past six they return to their tea,
Of a kind that would hardly be tempting to me,
    Though my appetite passes belief.
There is Jam, Ginger Beer, Buttered Toast,
                               Marmalade,
With Cold Leg of Mutton and Warm Lemonade,
And a large Pigeon Pie very skilfully made
    To consist almost wholly of Beef.

MORAL

A Respectable Family taking the air
  Is a subject on which I could dwell;
It contains all the morals that ever there were,
  And it sets an example as well.

stands for Gnu,
  whose weapons of Defence
Are long, sharp, curling Horns, and
  Common-sense,
To these he adds a Name so short and strong,

That even Hardy Boers pronounce it wrong.

How often on a bright Autumnal day
The Pious people of Pretoria say,
"Come, let us hunt the—" Then no more is
                                    heard
But Sounds of Strong Men struggling with a
                                    word.
Meanwhile, the distant Gnu with grateful eyes
Observes his opportunity, and flies.

MORAL

Child, if you have a rummy kind of name,
Remember to be thankful for the same.

H was a Horseman

who rode to the meet,
And talked of the Pads of the fox as his "feet" –
An error which furnished subscribers with grounds
For refusing to make him a Master of Hounds.

He gave way thereupon to so fearful a rage,
That he sold up his Stable and went on the Stage,
And had all the success that a man could desire
In creating the Part of
"The Old English Squire."

MORAL

In the Learned Professions, a person should
know
The advantage of having two strings to his bow.

I

The Poor Indian, justly called "The Poor,"
He has to eat his Dinner off the floor

MORAL

The Moral these delightful lines afford
Is: "Living cheaply is its own reward."

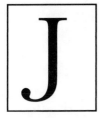

J stands for James,
      who thought it immaterial
To pay his taxes, Local or Imperial.
In vain the Mother wept, the Wife implored,
James only yawned as though a trifle bored.

The Tax Collector called again, but he
Was met with Persiflage and Repartee.

When James was hauled before the learned
Judge,
Who lectured him, he loudly whispered,
"Fudge!"

The Judge was startled from his usual calm,
He struck the desk before him with his palm,
And roared in tones to make the boldest quail,
"*J stands for James*, IT ALSO STANDS FOR JAIL."

And therefore, on a dark and dreadful day,
Policemen came and took him all away.

MORAL

The fate of James is typical, and shows
   How little mercy people can expect
Who will not pay their taxes; (saving those
   To which they conscientiously object).

for the Klondyke,
        a Country of Gold,

Where the winters are often excessively cold;
Where the lawn every morning is covered
                         with rime,
And skating continues for years at a time.
Do you think that a Climate can conquer the
                            grit
Of the Sons of the West? Not a bit! Not a bit!

When the weather looks nippy, the bold
                              Pioneers
Put on two pairs of Stockings and cover
                             their ears,
And roam through the drear Hyperborean
                               dales
With a vast apparatus of Buckets and Pails;

Or wander through wild Hyperborean glades
With Hoes, Hammers, Pickaxes, Mattocks
                        and Spades.

There are some who give rise to exuberant
                                                    mirth
By turning up nothing but bushels of earth,
While those who have little cause excellent fun
By attempting to pilfer from those who have
                                                    none.
At times the reward they will get for their pains
Is to strike very tempting auriferous veins;
Or, a shaft being sunk for some miles in the
                                                    ground,
Not infrequently nuggets of value are found.
They bring us the gold when their labours
                                                    are ended,
And we – after thanking them prettily –
                                                    spend it.

MORAL
Just you work for Humanity, never you mind
If Humanity seems to have left you behind.

was a Lady,

       Advancing in Age,

Who drove in her carriage and six,

With a Couple of Footmen, a Coachman

              and Page,

  Who were all of them regular bricks.

If the Coach ran away, or was smashed by a Dray,

  Or got into collisions and blocks,

The Page, with a courtesy rare for his years,

Would leap to the ground with inspiriting cheers,

While the Footman allayed her legitimate fears,

  And the Coachman sat tight on his box.

At night as they met round an excellent meal,
    They would take it in turn to observe:
"What a Lady indeed! . . . what a presence
                                to feel! . . ."
"What a Woman to worship and serve! . . ."

But, perhaps, the most poignant of all their
                                delights
    Was to stand in a rapturous Dream
When she spoke to them kindly on Saturday
                                Nights,
    And said "They deserved her Esteem."

MORAL

Now observe the Reward of these dutiful lives:
    At the end of their Loyal Career
They each had a Lodge at the end of the drives,
    And she left them a Hundred a Year.
Remember from this to be properly vexed
    When the newspaper editors say,
That "The type of society shown in the Text
    Is rapidly passing away."

was a Millionaire
                    who sat at Table,
        And ate like this –

                        as long as he was able;
        At half-past twelve the waiters turned him out:
            He lived impoverished and died of gout.

MORAL

Disgusting exhibition! Have a care
When, later on you are a Millionaire,
To rise from table feeling you could still
Take something more, and not be really ill.

stands for Ned,
Maria's younger brother,
Who, walking one way, chose to gaze the other.

In Blandford Square – a crowded part of town –
Two people on a tandem knocked him down:

Whereat

a Motor Car, with warning shout
Ran right on top and turned him inside out:
The damages that he obtained from these
Maintained him all his life in cultured ease.

MORAL

The law protects you. Go your gentle way:
The Other Man has always got to Pay.

stands for Oxford.

         Hail! salubrious seat
Of learning! Academical Retreat!
Home of my Middle Age! Malarial Spot
Which People call Medeeval (though it's not).
The marshes in the neighbourhood can vie
With Cambridge, but the town itself is dry,
And serves to make a kind of Fold or Pen

Wherein to herd a lot of Learned Men.

Were I to write but half of what they know,
It would exhaust the space reserved for "O";
And, as my book must not be over big,
I turn at once to "P," which stands for Pig.

MORAL

Be taught by this to speak with moderation
Of places where, with decent application,
One gets a good, sound, middle-class education.

stands for Pig,
　　　　as I remarked before,

A second cousin to the Huge Wild Boar.
But Pigs are civilised, while Huge Wild Boars

Live savagely, at random, out of doors,
And, in their coarse contempt for dainty foods,
Subsist on Truffles, which they find in woods.
Not so the cultivated Pig, who feels
The need of several courses at his meals,
But wrongly thinks it does not matter whether

He takes them one by one

or all together.
Hence, Pigs devour, from lack of self-respect,
What Epicures would certainly eject.

MORAL

Learn from the Pig to take whatever Fate
Or Elder Persons heap upon your plate.

Q for Quinine,

which children take
With Jam and little bits of cake.

MORAL

How idiotic! Can Quinine
Replace Cold Baths and Sound Hygiene?

the Reviewer,

reviewing my book,
At which he had barely intended to look;

But the very first lines upon "A" were enough
To convince him the *Verses* were excellent stuff.
So he wrote, without stopping, for several days
In terms of extreme but well-merited Praise.
To quote but one Passage: "No Person" (says he)
"Will be really content without purchasing three,
"While a Parent will send for a dozen or more,
"And strew them about on the Nursery Floor.
"The Versification might call for some strictures
"Were it not for its singular wit; while the
                                        Pictures,
"Tho' the handling of line is a little defective,
"Make up amply in *verve* what they lack in
                                        perspective."

MORAL
The habit of constantly telling the Truth
Will lend an additional lustre to Youth.

stands for Snail,

who, though he be the least,
Is not an uninstructive Hornèd Beast.

His eyes are on his Horns, and when you shout
Or tickle them, the Horns go in and out.
Had Providence seen proper to endow
The furious Unicorn or sober Cow
With such a gift, the one would never now
Appear so commonplace on Coats of Arms.
And what a fortune for our failing farms
If circus managers, with wealth untold,
Would take the Cows for half their weight
in gold!

MORAL

Learn from the Snail to take reproof with
patience,
And not put out your Horns on all occasions.

for the Genial Tourist,
who resides

In Peckham, where he writes Italian Guides.

MORAL

Learn from this information not to cavil
At slight mistakes in books on foreign travel.

339

U

for the Upas Tree,

that casts a blight
On those that pull their sisters' hair, and fight.

But oh! the Good! They wander undismayed.
And (as the Subtle Artist has portrayed)
Dispend the golden hours at play beneath its
shade.*

MORAL

Dear Reader, if you chance to catch a sight
Of Upas Trees, betake yourself to flight.

* A friend of mine, a Botanist, believes
  That Good can even browse upon its leaves.
  I doubt it . . .

for the unobtrusive Volunteer,

Who fills the Armies of the World with fear.

MORAL

Seek with the Volunteer to put aside
The empty Pomp of Military Pride.

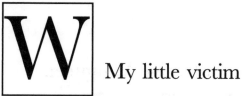

My little victim

let me trouble you
To fix your active mind on W.

343

The WATERBEETLE here shall teach
A sermon far beyond your reach:
He flabbergasts the Human Race
By gliding on the water's face
With ease, celerity, and grace;
But if he ever stopped to think
Of how he did it, he would sink.

MORAL
Don't ask Questions!

No reasonable little Child expects
A Grown-up Man to make a rhyme on X.

MORAL
These verses teach a clever child to find
Excuse for doing all that he's inclined.

stands for Youth

(it would have stood for Yak,
But that I wrote about him two years back).

Youth is the pleasant springtime of our days,
As Dante so mellifluously says
(Who always speaks of Youth with proper
                                    praise).
You have not got to Youth, but when you do
You'll find what He and I have said is true.

MORAL
Youth's excellence should teach the Modern Wit
First to be Young, and then to boast of it.

Z for this Zébu,

who (like all Zebús)*
Is held divine by scrupulous Hindoos.

* Von Kettner writes it "Zébu"; Wurst "Zebu"
  I split the difference and use the two.

348

MORAL

Idolatry, as you are aware,
Is highly reprehensible. But there,
We needn't bother – when we get to Z
Our interest in the Alphabet is dead.